MOBILE SERVICES

THUNDER BUNNY

BARBARA HELEN BERGER

PHILOMEL BOOKS

Thunder Bunny was a surprise.

Even her own mama said, "Oh, my."

She was the last and littlest one.
Soon she could flick her ears
and jump and thump and dig in the dirt
like all the others.

But there was something about her.
Just . . . something.

"Well of course," said old Granny,
"she came out of the blue."

"I did?"

Thunder Bunny looked up at the sky.

She saw the sun, and she saw the moon,
and she wondered.
She saw the clouds come and go—

and the blue was always there,
no matter what.
She said, "I came from the sky."

"Oh, pooh," said the others.
"You're only a bunny.
Bunnies don't come from the sky!"
"Well, *I* do."

Just then,
a wind came rushing over the grass.
The others ran to hide.

But Thunder Bunny said,
"I will jump on the wind!"
So she did.

And the wind carried her up, up,
high above the hill.

"I am the blue and the blue is me!"
She felt so free, she wanted to leap
all the way to the sun and the moon.

But a cloud billowed up in her way,
so big, it covered the blue.
Thunder Bunny said,
"I will dig a hole through."

So she dug and she dug,
and the hole became a tunnel.
The deeper she dug, the darker it was.
The cloud began to rumble.

Thunder Bunny stopped.
She was afraid
in the rumbling dark
and far from home.
She sat very still.
Her own heart was thumping.

Then she thought,
"I am the blue."

She flicked her ears.
"I am the blue and the blue is me!"
She thumped her feet in the tunnel.
"I am a rumble bunny."
She thumped even louder.
"I am a Thun-Thun-*Thunder* Bunny!"

BOOM.
The cloud broke open.
Rain poured down.

Below in the burrow,
the others huddled and cuddled.

Where was the littlest one?

"Mama, she never came in!"
"She must be sopping wet
and scared silly," Mama said.
Off they ran to find her.

Soon, not a shadow of cloud was left,
not a whiffle of wind.
But the sky was still there.
And up on the hill,
they found a glorious rabbit.
The light of her dazzled their eyes.

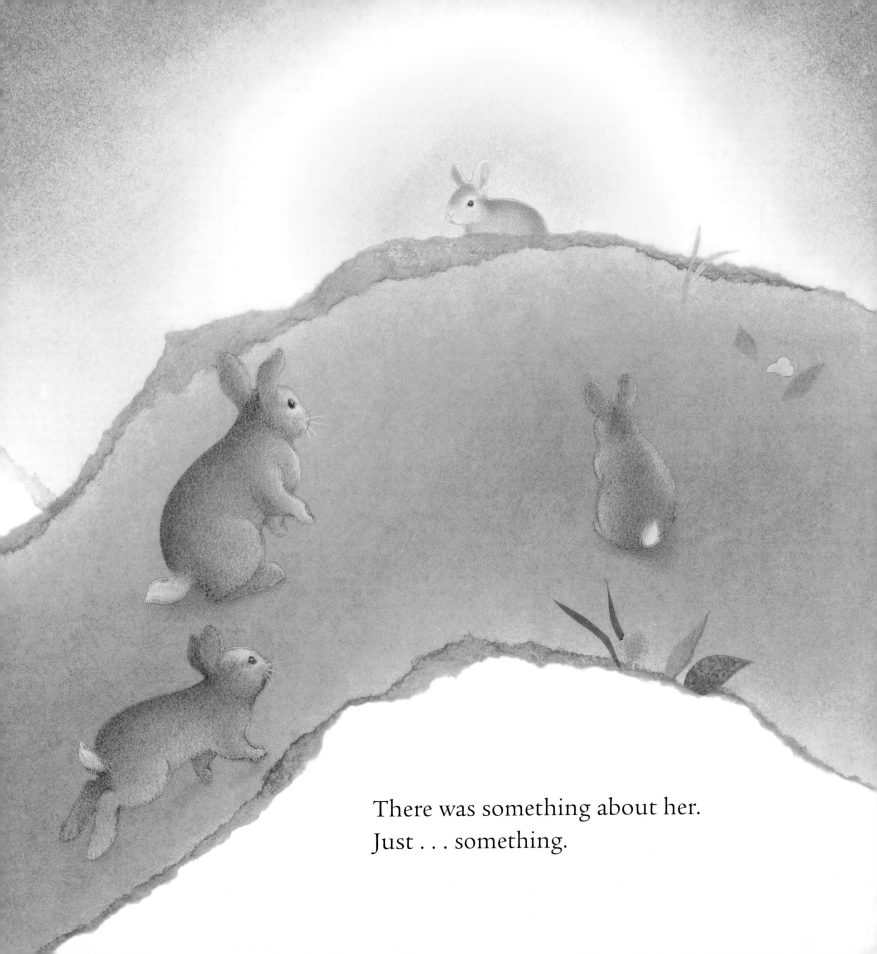

There was something about her.
Just . . . something.

"Thunder Bunny, is that you?"
She wasn't *only* a bunny now.
She was a sun and moon bunny,
clear and true and out of the blue,
the blue that is always there,
no matter what.
"Yes," she said. "Here I am."

They all
cuddled around her in the quiet.
Even her own mama said, "Oh, my."

To Amaya

Patricia Lee Gauch, editor

PHILOMEL BOOKS

A division of Penguin Young Readers Group.
Published by The Penguin Group.
Penguin Group (USA) Inc., 375 Hudson Street, New York, NY 10014, U.S.A.
Penguin Group (Canada), 90 Eglinton Avenue East, Suite 700, Toronto, Ontario, Canada M4P 2Y3 (a division of Pearson Penguin Canada Inc.).
Penguin Books Ltd, 80 Strand, London WC2R 0RL, England.
Penguin Ireland, 25 St. Stephen's Green, Dublin 2, Ireland (a division of Penguin Books Ltd.).
Penguin Group (Australia), 250 Camberwell Road, Camberwell, Victoria 3124, Australia (a division of Pearson Australia Group Pty Ltd).
Penguin Books India Pvt Ltd, 11 Community Centre, Panchsheel Park, New Delhi - 110 017, India.
Penguin Group (NZ), Cnr Airborne and Rosedale Roads, Albany, Auckland 1310, New Zealand (a division of Pearson New Zealand Ltd).
Penguin Books (South Africa) (Pty) Ltd, 24 Sturdee Avenue, Rosebank, Johannesburg 2196, South Africa.
Penguin Books Ltd, Registered Offices: 80 Strand, London WC2R 0RL, England.

Design by Semadar Megged.   Text set in Legacy Serif.   The collage illustrations were done in pastel on torn and cut paper, bonded with
polymer medium and heat, then refined with acrylic for detail.

Library of Congress Cataloging-in-Publication Data
Berger, Barbara Helen, 1945 Mar. 1–   Thunder Bunny / Barbara Helen Berger.   p. cm.   Summary: Bright blue and different from all her
brothers and sisters, Thunder Bunny discovers she came from the sky.   [1. Individuality—Fiction. 2. Sky—Fiction. 3. Rabbits—Fiction.] I. Title.
PZ7.B4513Th 2007   [E]—dc22   2006008242   ISBN 978-0-399-22035-7
1 3 5 7 9 10 8 6 4 2
First Impression

For Kieran, James, and Hayden   S.J.D.

To every child in the world deprived of
a peaceful and happy Christmas   D.K.

Text copyright © 2009 Sarah J. Dodd
Illustrations copyright © 2009 Dubravka Kolanovic
This edition copyright © 2009 Lion Hudson

The moral rights of the author and illustrator
have been asserted

A Lion Children's Book
an imprint of
Lion Hudson plc
Wilkinson House, Jordan Hill Road,
Oxford OX2 8DR, England
www.lionhudson.com
UK ISBN 978 0 7459 6917 6
US ISBN 978 0 8254 7950 2

First edition 2009
This printing July 2009
10 9 8 7 6 5 4 3 2 1 0

A catalogue record for this book is available
from the British Library

Typeset in 18/23 Goudy Old Style BT
Printed and bound in China by Printplus Ltd

Distributed by:
UK: Marston Book Services Ltd,
PO Box 269, Abingdon, Oxon OX14 4YN
USA: Trafalgar Square Publishing,
814 N Franklin Street, Chicago, IL 60610
USA Christian Market: Kregel Publications,
PO Box 2607, Grand Rapids, MI 49501

Christmas Stories for
Little Angels

Sarah J. Dodd

Dubravka Kolanovic

LION
CHILDREN'S

Mary's surprise

Mary was a good girl, just grown up. She lived with her parents and always did as they asked. They gave her everything she needed. They had found a fine man called Joseph for her to marry. Mary liked to know what would happen from one day to the next. She didn't like surprises.

One morning, Mary was sweeping the floor. Suddenly a bright light appeared in the corner. Mary gasped and dropped her broom.

"Don't be afraid," said a voice. An angel stepped forward. "God has sent me with a message. He would like you to be the mother of his child. It will be a boy, and his name will be Jesus."

"It's a nice name," said Mary, "but the whole idea is a big surprise. I'll have to think about it."

Mary thought hard. What would happen if she did as God asked?

Her parents might think she was bad; her friends might think she was mad; and Joseph would be so, so sad.
She would have to say no.
"God would be very glad," said the angel.

Mary looked out of the window. She thought of the way her parents smiled when she pleased them. She wondered how God's smile might look.

Mary looked back at the angel. "I will do what God has asked me," she said.

"Thank you," said the angel. "God will be so pleased. And one day, so will people all over the world."

The angel disappeared. Mary took a deep breath, then she went outside. It was time to share the surprise with Joseph.

Bad news, good news

Joseph couldn't get to sleep. He tossed and twisted, fretted and fidgeted. He counted camels backwards in his head. But his eyes stayed wide open.

"Such bad news," he muttered. "I can't marry Mary now."

At last, Joseph fell asleep. He dreamed that a bright angel sat on the stool by his bed.

"This is a very good seat," said the angel. "Did you make it yourself?"

Joseph's mouth fell open. He nodded.

"I thought so. God told me that you take care over everything you do. That's why God chose you."

"Chose me for what? I've got enough to think about without making more furniture," Joseph grumbled.

"What's the matter?" asked the angel.
"I've had some bad news," sighed Joseph. "Mary is having a baby. I don't know who its father is."

"I've got good news!" said the angel. "God is the baby's father, but he would like you to take care of it for him."

"I don't think I'd be any good at that job," said Joseph. "I've never been a Dad before."

"God will help you," said the angel.

The dream was so real that Joseph woke with a jump. He knew what he must do.

Joseph raced round to Mary's house and banged on the door. "I need to see Mary," he shouted.

Mary's father threw open the window. "She's asleep in bed," he growled. "Like we all were."

"No, I'm not." Mary appeared at the door.

Joseph threw his arms round her. "Mary, will you still marry me?"

"Of course I will," she said.

Journey to Bethlehem

"We have to go on a journey," said Joseph.
The donkey pricked up his ears.
"A journey?" said Mary.
"Everyone has to go back to their family home to be counted."
"But your family home is in Bethlehem. That's *miles* away!"
Mary frowned.
"You can ride on the donkey. He's good and strong."

The donkey looked at Mary. He looked at the enormous bump where the baby was growing inside her. His ears drooped.

The journey lasted for days. The donkey's feet were sore and his knees knocked together. He was ready for a rest.

Mary and Joseph were ready for a rest, too. But all the beds in Bethlehem were full.

The donkey nudged the door of a stable.

"I can't stay in *there*," wailed Mary. "What if my baby comes?"

"It's all we have," said Joseph. "I'll ask the owner if we can stay."

It was all agreed. The animals would have to squeeze up and make room. Mary sank into a pile of clean straw. The donkey dozed off.

When the donkey woke up, light filled the stable. Mary and Joseph were gazing towards the manger. A baby lay on the hay.

The donkey knew there was something special about the baby. He forgot his aching knees and knelt down.

"The angel told me to call him Jesus," whispered Mary.

Joseph nodded and smiled. "I'll take good care of him," he said.

The smallest shepherd

Simon was learning to be a shepherd. Tonight was the first time he had stayed out all night.

"Don't be afraid," he whispered to the lamb on his knee. "I'll take care of you." He huddled closer to the fire.

"Not scared, are you?" laughed Judah.

Simon shook his head. But the field beyond the reach of the firelight looked darker than ever.

"I'm not afraid of anything," boasted Judah.

"Shepherds don't shake," agreed Daniel.

Simon shivered and wished he was brave like his brothers.

Suddenly the sky exploded with light.

"Help!" shrieked Judah, and he fell to the ground.

"Save me!" screamed Daniel, and he dived behind a bush.

Simon peered through his fingers. An angel smiled down
at him, brighter than fifty fires.

"Don't be afraid," said the angel. "This very night, a baby has
been born in Bethlehem. He is God's Son, and he will bring joy
to the world."

Simon dared to take his hands away from his eyes. Angels filled the sky, all singing for joy. Simon gazed at them and felt brave from his toes to the top of his head.

All at once, the angels disappeared. Simon looked up at the sky, ablaze with stars. "You know what?" he murmured, kissing the lamb's woolly head. "I don't think I'll ever be afraid again."

Heavenly hallelujah

The streets of Bethlehem were dark, but one small stable was lit up like a lantern. As the shepherds raced towards it, Simon recognized the flare of gold around the roof.

"That's angel light!" he breathed.

When the shepherds reached the stable, they hung back, suddenly shy.

"Smallest first," said Judah, prodding Simon in the back.

Simon tiptoed into the stable and peered into the rough wooden manger. An ordinary-looking baby lay in it, wrapped up snug and warm, and fast asleep. But Simon remembered the words of the angel. This was no ordinary baby. This was God's Son.

Simon elbowed Daniel and Judah aside. He dashed out into the quiet streets.

"Wake up!" he yelled. "Something amazing has happened!"

Lamps flickered and voices murmured as Simon ran up and down, shouting out the exciting news.

People appeared in doorways, children rubbing sleep from their eyes. In ones and twos, holding the little ones by the hand, they followed Simon to the stable. The children squeezed in, giggling and whispering. More angels gathered, singing a heavenly hallelujah.

The baby slept on, smiling in his sleep as though the whole world had been made for him.

Jasper's new friend

Jasper was tired of looking after grumpy camels. He was tired of sleeping on the ground and missed his cosy hayloft above the camel stable. Cooking smells drifted from the village, and Jasper imagined families laughing together over their meal.

He couldn't remember his own family. Jasper was the least important of the camel keepers. Everyone ignored him, especially the wise men, who were in charge of this trip. They were busy watching the star. It was their idea to follow it all this way. Jasper took his toy camel from beneath his cloak. She had been his friend since he was tiny. He hugged her and blinked his tears away.

"That's the place!" shouted one of the wise men, pointing.
The star hung above a small house, up the hill in Bethlehem.
Jasper sighed, got up and untied the camels.
The journey wasn't over yet.

When they reached the house, the wise men went in. Jasper peered round the door. A young couple sat inside, a baby crawling at their feet.

The wise men offered the baby expensive, but grown-up, presents – gold, frankincense and myrrh. The mother smiled and thanked them.

But the baby spotted Jasper. Gurgling, he crawled towards the door and lifted his chubby hands.

"I haven't brought you a present," whispered Jasper.

The baby pointed at the toy camel.

Jasper shook his head. "She's my special friend. She's my *only* friend."

The baby hugged Jasper's leg. Nobody had hugged Jasper in a long time.

Jasper crouched down and held out his camel.

The baby took it, and smiled at Jasper as though he was the most important person in the world. And Jasper knew that he had found a true friend.